Usborne
Stories
for Little
Children

Usborne
Stories
for Little
Children

Contents

6

The Gingerbread Man

Once upon a time, many years ago,

a little old woman

and a little old man
lived on a farm.

They were kind people.

It made them sad that they had no children.

"If only we had a little boy," sighed the little old woman.

"I know!" she said one day.
"I could make a boy out
of gingerbread!"

So she took out her recipe book.

She weighed and she measured,

she mixed and she stirred,

she rolled the dough and she cut out a shape.

Then she put it in the oven to bake.

13

Soon the kitchen was filled with the smell of hot gingerbread.

"Almost ready now," said the little old woman,
and she opened the oven to look.

Mmmm...

Out jumped a little gingerbread man!

He pattered across
the kitchen floor...

...and ran right out
of the open door!

"Stop!" called the little old woman.

"Stop, stop!" called the little old man.

But the gingerbread man
ran along the road, singing:

Run, run, as fast as you can,
You can't catch me
I'm the gingerbread man!

He raced past a horse
and a cow, grazing in the meadow.

"Mmm, you look delicious,"
neighed the horse.

"Come here, little man," mooed the cow.

17

But the gingerbread man ran along the road, singing:

I have run away from a little old woman and a little old man,
and I can run away from you too, yes I can!

Run, run, as fast as you can,
You can't catch me
I'm the gingerbread man!

He sped past a farmer,
hard at work in a field.

"Mmm, what a treat,"
said the farmer.
"Come here, little man."

But the gingerbread man ran along the road, singing:

I have run away from a horse, a cow,
a little old woman and a little old man,
and I can run away from you too, yes I can!

Run, run, as fast as you can,

You can't catch me
I'm the gingerbread man!

He scampered past a school,

and all the children shouted,
"Mmm, we love gingerbread!
Come here, little man!"

But the gingerbread man ran along the road, singing:

I have run away from a farmer in a field, a horse, a cow,
a little old woman and a little old man,
and I can run away from you too, yes I can!

Run, run, as fast as you can,

You can't catch me

I'm the gingerbread man!

On and on he ran,
until he came to a river.

He wanted to cross it, but
he was afraid of getting wet.

A fox spotted him.
"If you climb onto my
tail, I'll help you across,"
he said.

The fox started swimming with the gingerbread man on his tail.

Soon, though, his tail was dragging in the water.

"I'm so sorry," said the fox.

"Do climb onto my back."

But soon the water was lapping over the fox's back.

"I'm so sorry," said the fox.
"Do climb onto my head."

The gingerbread man tiptoed
up to the fox's head...

28

The fox tossed his head, and SNAP!
The gingerbread man was a quarter gone.

SNAP! He was half gone.

SNAP! Three quarters gone...

29

SNAP! And that was the end of him.

Quack! Quack!

The Nutcracker

It was Christmas Eve.
The world was
covered in a crisp
blanket of snow.

Everything was dazzling white,
except for the golden light
that spilled out from
Clara's house.

Inside, a party was in full swing.
Clara stared out of the window...

She was waiting for something
magical to happen.

Suddenly,
the door burst open.

Merry Christmas, Clara!

It was her godfather.

"I've brought you a
wonderful present,"
he said.

To Clara,
This present isn't all
that it seems...
From your Godfather

"What can it be?"
wondered Clara, as she
lay in bed that night.

She was so excited,
she couldn't wait
to find out.

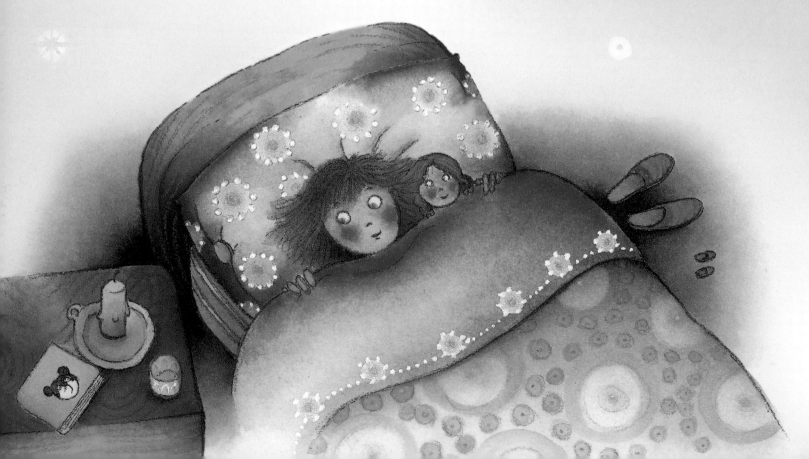

Clara ran downstairs...
and ripped off the wrapping paper.

Inside was a
nutcracker toy.

Clara hugged him tight and
curled up under the tree. Soon,
she was fast asleep.

39

Dong! Dong! The clock struck midnight. Clara woke with a start. There was a great whooshing sound.

The Christmas tree was rising up above her.

What's happening?

"Hello Clara," whispered a voice behind her.

"My nutcracker?" gasped Clara. He bowed. "I'm the Nutcracker Prince," he said.

41

"I've come to protect you.
The kitchen mice are plotting
to kidnap you."

He blew sharply on his whistle
and six soldiers marched
out of the toy box.

They were just in time. The kitchen
mice stormed out of the shadows.

The soldiers struck them down with lumps
of cheese and sprayed them with water.

"Is cheese the best you can do?" jeered an evil voice. It was the Mouse King.

He whipped out his sword and lunged at the Nutcracker Prince.

CLASH! CLANG!
went their swords.
"I must help!"
thought Clara.

She took off her slipper
and threw it.

Weeeeeeeeeeeeeeeeeee!

It whizzed through the
air and knocked the King out cold.

47

"You were brilliant!" said the Nutcracker Prince.
"Now we must celebrate."

He called for his reindeer and his magical, golden sleigh.
Clara and the Prince climbed aboard.

They flew through an open window and into
the snow-filled sky.

The reindeer rode through the night.
Far below, Clara could see lollipop trees
and marshmallow flowers.

"Welcome to the Land of Sweets,"

announced the Prince.

They rode up to a marzipan castle,
decorated with all kinds of treats.

"I'm so glad you've come," said a dazzling fairy, dancing out to greet them.

I am the Sugarplum Fairy. Come inside and eat.

52

Clara and the Prince
sat down to a feast of
cookies and cakes
and candy swirls.

Then they watched dances
from around the world.
Spinning Spanish dancers
clicked their castanets.

53

Arabian princesses swirled...

...Chinese tea dancers whirled...

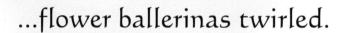

...flower ballerinas twirled.

Clara watched, enchanted.

But the slow, soothing music called her to sleep. "It's time to go home," whispered the Nutcracker Prince.

When Clara woke up, she was under the Christmas tree once more and the Prince had gone.

"He's only a wooden toy!" cried Clara. "Was it a dream? Or was it the magic of Christmas Eve?"

To Clara,
This present isn't all
that it seems...
From your Godfat

The Story of Pinocchio

Gepetto the carpenter had always wanted to make a puppet. One day, he found the perfect piece of wood.

He began by carving a
head and a little nose.

Slowly, the nose grew...

longer...

and longer...

and longer.

Gepetto was
astonished,
but he kept
on carving.

Hours later, he finished his long-nosed puppet and smiled.

Suddenly, the puppet jumped up, snatched Gepetto's wig and ran outside.

"Come back here, puppet!"
Gepetto cried.

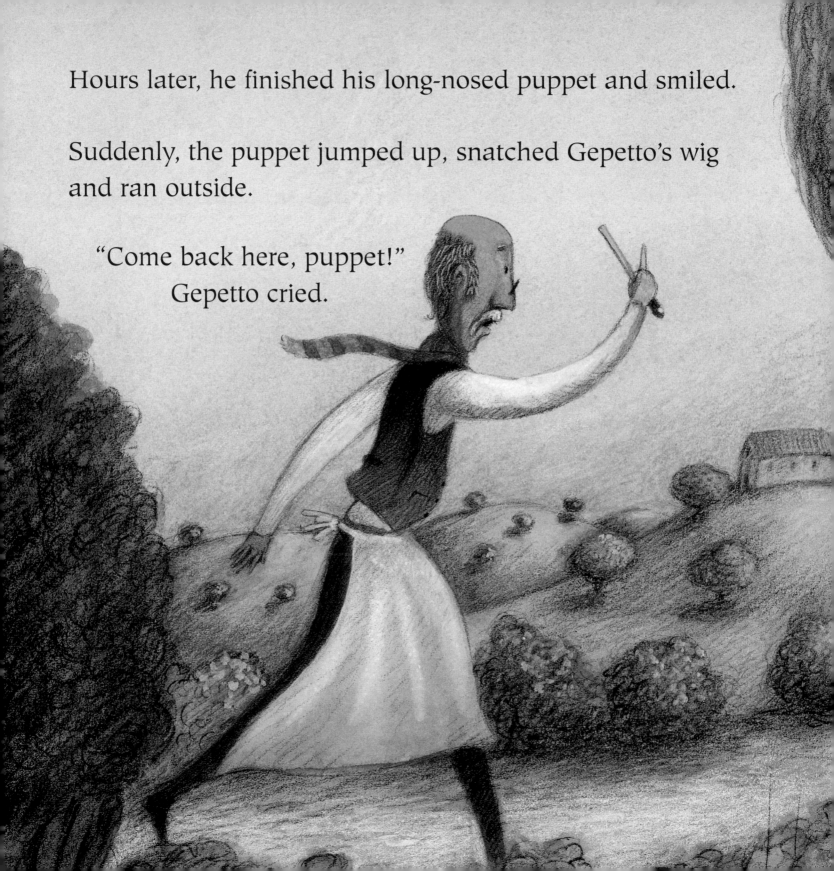

"I'm not a puppet," it shouted.
"My name is Pinocchio and I'm
a *real* boy."

Pinocchio kept running,
straight past a
policeman.

"What's going on?" asked the policeman.
Then he saw Gepetto waving a chisel.
"Stop there, old man," he ordered. "You look dangerous."

"Tee hee," giggled
Pinocchio. He skipped
home and snuggled by the fire.

Buzzzzzzzzzzzzzzz...

"Foolish puppet,"
buzzed a cricket.

62

"Hey!" shouted Pinocchio. "I'm not a puppet. I'm a *real* boy."

"You're not," said the cricket. "You're a naughty puppet. Only good puppets become real boys."

Pinocchio was lost in thought...

until Gepetto arrived home with some supper.

"Er... Dad," said Pinocchio.
"I want to be a real boy."

Gepetto smiled.
"Well, let's start by
sending you to school."

Be good,
Pinocchio!

65

On the way to school, Pinocchio saw a crowd of people.

"Are you here for the puppet show?"
asked a well-dressed man.

"A puppet show?" said Pinocchio. "Oh yes!"

He sold his school book, bought a ticket...

...and dashed into the show.

"Hello puppet," the performers called to
Pinocchio. "Come and join us."

"We're going to the
Land of Lost Toys,"
said a clown. "Do
you want to come?"

"I'd love to!"
said Pinocchio.

The Land of Lost Toys was one big funfair.

"Yippeeeeee!" squealed Pinocchio.

"Are you a lost toy too?"
asked a teddy bear.

"Um... yes," lied Pinocchio.
His wooden nose began to itch.

"I have no family," said the teddy bear.
"Nor do I," lied Pinocchio.

His itchy nose began to grow.

It grew

longer

and **longer**.

"Foolish puppet,"
buzzed a voice. "Your
father is sick with worry.
He's rowing across the ocean
to find you."

"Oh no!" Pinocchio said. "I must save him."
Instantly, his nose began to shrink.

"I'll help," cooed a pigeon.

Pinocchio jumped on her back
and they soared to the coast.

Pinocchio?
Where are you?

"There he is!"
cried Pinocchio.

As the puppet watched, a huge wave rose up and swallowed Gepetto's boat.

"I'll save you, Dad!" called Pinocchio, diving into the chilly water.

Pinocchio swam and swam... but there was no sign of Gepetto.

Then he felt a rush of water and everything went dark.

"Where am I?" wondered Pinocchio, with a shudder. Peering into the gloom, he saw a faint glow.

He followed it down a squelchy tunnel...

SQUELCH SQUELCH

...and stopped in surprise.

An old man was sitting at a desk.
"Dad?" whispered Pinocchio.

Pinocchio!

"I'm sorry I was so naughty," said Pinocchio.
"But don't worry, I'll get us out of here."

Pinocchio led Gepetto back along the dark, squelchy tunnel, to the mouth of a cave.

"Jump!" cried Pinocchio. "I'll tow you to the shore."

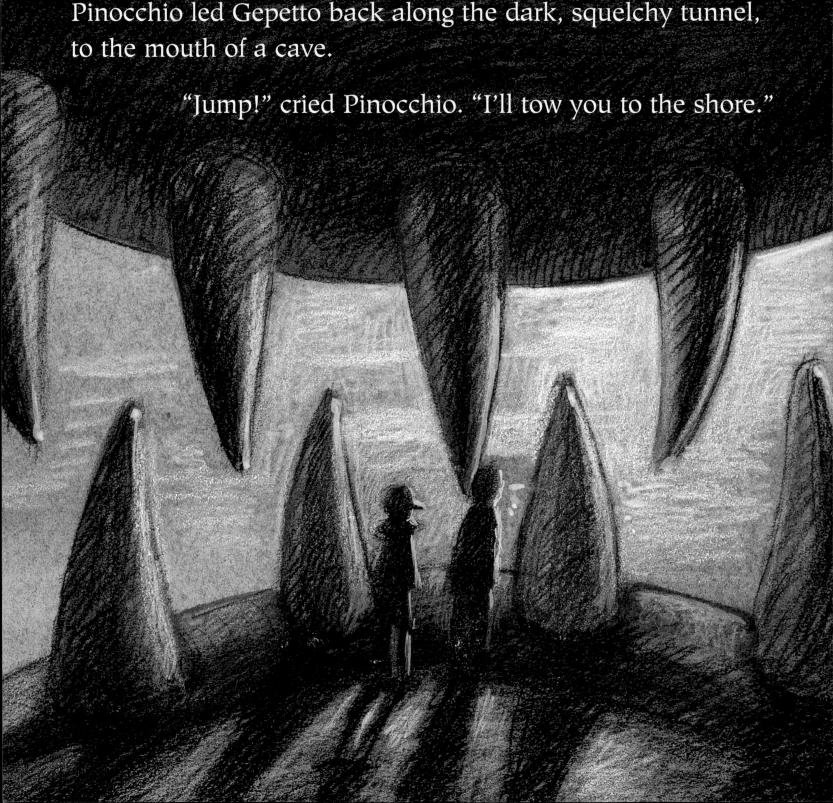

By midnight, Pinocchio and Gepetto were safely home.
"You're a good puppet," said Gepetto, kissing his son goodnight.

The next morning, Pinocchio woke up
feeling very different...

He was a real
boy at last.

The Town Mouse and the Country Mouse

In among the waving grasses,

lies a little brown country mouse, fast asleep.
His name is Pipin.

He dreams of crunchy seeds
and juicy red strawberries.

83

Every evening Pipin
pattered home

to his little house
in the leafy hedge.

Then, one cold winter's day, there was
a RAT-A-TAT-TAT at his door.

"Pipin!" cried a voice.
It was Toby Town Mouse, come to stay.

"Oh my whiskers!" cried Pipin.
He rushed to his pantry for his best nuts and berries.

"Is this all you have?"
asked Toby Town Mouse.

"In town we eat like kings.
I think you'd better come and stay with me."

The mice scampered to the station early next morning.

The train trundled in with a snort and a shriek.

"It's HUGE!" gasped Pipin.
"It's like a **big**
red
beast."

They wriggled inside a man's
green bag and were lifted aboard. Then...

89

Chugga-chugga-chugga. Choo! Choo!
They were off!

Pipin gazed out of the window,
at trees waving their branches.

Then there were no trees at all –
just tall buildings that touched the sky.

"At last!" cried Toby, sniffing the air. "We're here!"

Hurry up, Pipin!

They ran out of the station onto a busy street.

"Help!" squeaked Pipin, dodging in and out of stamping feet.

92

"This is it," said Toby, proudly pointing his paw. "My house."
They crept through a crack under the blue front door.

Toby led Pipin down under the floor,
up secret stairs behind the walls

and into a splendid dining hall.

The mice nibbled
and gnawed

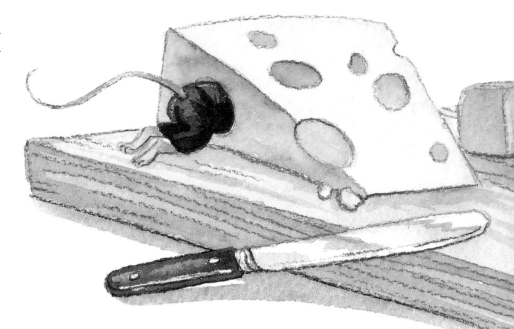

and scooped cream
with their paws,

until they were
perfectly full.

They woke with a start as the table shook.

"MY dinner time!"
purred the kitchen cat.

Mmmmm...
Juicy little mice.

"Run!" squeaked Toby.

The mice darted
this way
and that.

Pounce! Pounce!
went the hungry cat.

She swiped at Pipin
with her pointy claws.

Quick, Pipin! Into this hole.

Pipin ran.

The cat leaped...

...and missed.

"Curses!" she hissed.

99

"Oh my whiskers," said Pipin, mopping his brow.
"I want to go home."

Oh! Why?

"This town life is too much for me."

Toby took Pipin to the station
and waved goodbye.

Pipin gazed again
as tall buildings
flashed quickly
past his eyes.

101

In the starry dark, Pipin
finally reached his hedge.

He sniffed the cold, sweet air and smiled.

Then he snuggled down
in his soft, mossy bed.

"This is the life for me," Pipin said.

104

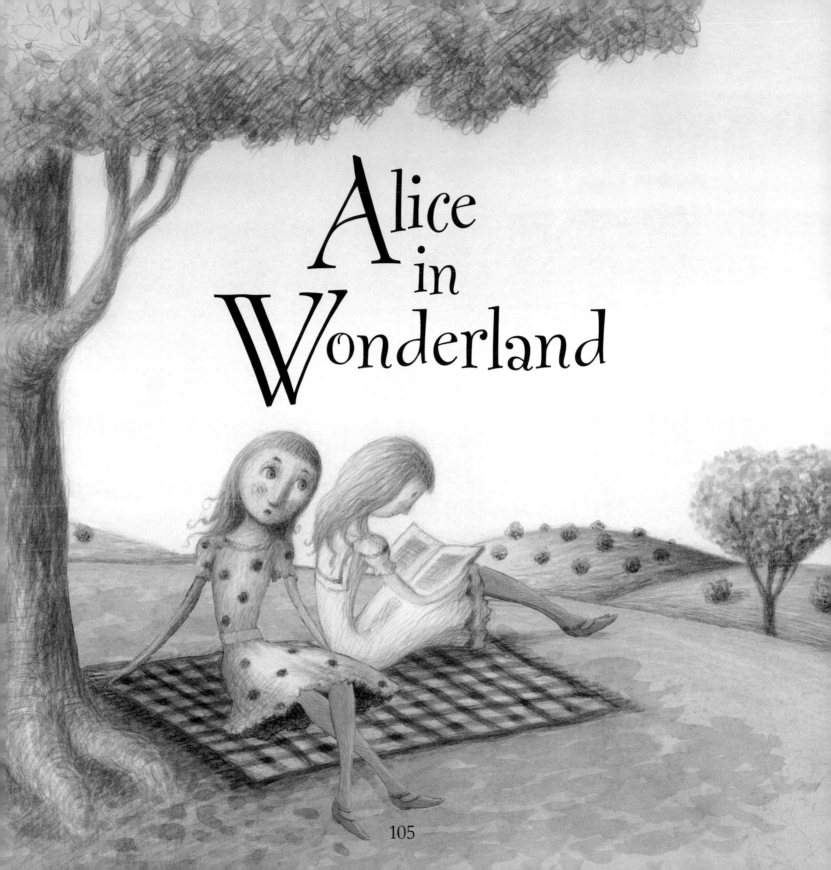

Alice in Wonderland

Alice's sister was deep in her book
and Alice was feeling bored.

All at once, she saw
a White Rabbit
with a pocket watch.

"Whoever heard of a rabbit with a pocket –
or a watch?" thought Alice...

...so she followed him

down

    into

       his

         hole.

D
o
w
n
D
o
w
n
D
o
w
n

Alice thought the hole would never end, until she landed – with a BUMP.

She was in a hall, looking onto a beautiful garden. But she was much too big to fit through the door.

Sunlight glinted on a glass bottle in the hall.

"Falling down holes is thirsty work,"
thought Alice. She took a great big gulp...

...and shrank to the size of a mouse.
Now she could go into the garden!

She was walking past a curly table leg, heading
for the tiny door, when she
saw a cake.

"Eat me!"
it said.

Eat Me

111

Alice bit into sticky icing... and shot up so quickly, her head hit the ceiling.

Now she was far too tall for anything.

Alice started to cry.

Huge, salty tears splashed onto the floor.

Just then, the White Rabbit ran past in a fluster.

"Oh my ears and whiskers, I'll be late!"

he gasped, dropping his fan.

Alice scooped it up...
and shrank again.

With a *splish* she tumbled into her salty lake of tears.

Peculiar creatures crowded around her.

"Swim for the shore!" they cried, so Alice swam.

114

"Shall I tell you a story?" she began,
as they dried off. "It's about my cat—"

"CAT?" they squawked and
hurried away, in a flurry
of wings and a scurry
of claws.

Left all alone, Alice wandered along until she met
a grumpy-looking caterpillar.

"Who are you?" he said.

"I don't know," sighed Alice. "I keep growing
and shrinking and it's all very confusing."

"Try eating some of my mushroom," said the caterpillar.

Alice nibbled a piece.

In a blink, the caterpillar vanished and a grinning cat appeared. Alice was baffled – and totally lost. "Where do I go now?" she asked.

"*That* way for the Hatter and *that* way for the March Hare," said the cat.

"I think I'll visit the Hare," thought Alice.
The Hatter had thought the same. She found them
both, drinking tea and talking nonsense.

"Why is a raven like a writing desk?"

Alice grew more
confused every second.

"This is the stupidest tea party ever!"
she said at last, running off.

"What party? And who are you?" snapped a voice. Alice had run slap-bang-wham into the Queen of Hearts.

"We're about to play a game," said the King, before
Alice could answer. "Won't you join us?"

It was the strangest game
Alice had ever seen.

Anyone who played badly was dragged
away by the Queen's guards.

124

"Everyone to court!" said the Queen, all of a sudden.
Alice followed behind but she was growing again.

"Off with her head!" shouted the Queen.

"Nonsense!" said Alice.

"You're nothing but a pack of cards!" she added.

Suddenly, everything whirled into the air,
spinning her around, faster and faster.

Alice shut her eyes tight.

When she opened them again,
all the cards had gone...

...and she was back at the
top of the rabbit hole.

128

"Curiouser and curiouser," said Alice,
and she went home for tea.

The Emperor's New Clothes

Once upon a time there was an
Emperor who loved clothes.

He liked looking splendid
ALL the time.

Don't I look splendid!

He had a different outfit for every day of the year.

But the Emperor had a problem. He had nothing to wear for the royal procession.

"Won't any of your outfits do, Your Highness?" asked his servant, Boris.

"NO!" said the Emperor.
"I want an outfit so splendid
that people will talk about me for years to come."

Boris sighed and set off to find the finest clothes-makers in town.

WANTED!
Splendid new outfit for the Emperor. Clothes-makers apply here!
NO TIME-WASTERS PLEASE

He wasn't having much luck until...

a little round man

and a long thin man
rushed up to him.

They bowed with their
bottoms in the air.
"We are Slimus and
Slick, at your service,"
they said.

Boris took them to the Emperor.

"We make magic clothes," Slimus told him.
"Only clever people can see them. Stupid people can't!"

"Are they splendid?" asked the Emperor.
"Very splendid," promised Slick. "But very expensive.
We'll need pots and pots of money."

"Take all the money you want," cried the Emperor.
"Just make me those clothes!"

A week later, the Emperor and Boris went to see
Slimus and Slick at work. "Welcome!" they said.
"What do you think of our clothes?"

The Emperor gulped. Boris gulped.
Neither of them could see a thing.

But they didn't want to look stupid.
So the Emperor said, "Splendid!"
"Yes, really very... splendid," said Boris.

"Oh, um, er, most splendid!" added the footmen.

Here! Have more money.

As soon as everyone had gone, Slimus and Slick laughed and laughed until their faces turned purple.

Then they ordered a huge feast.
"It's hungry work making magic clothes," they said.

On the morning of the royal procession,
the Emperor couldn't wait to put on his new clothes.

"Here is your cloak," said Slimus.
"It's light as a feather."

"Oh Your Highness," said Slick. "You look
very handsome. Your clothes fit so well."

The Emperor admired himself in the mirror. "Don't I look *splendid*?"

"Yes, Your Highness," gasped the footmen, staring straight at the Emperor.

"Yes, Your Highness," said Boris, staring straight at the ceiling. (He was trying NOT to look.)

"Open the palace gates!" ordered the Emperor. "Let the royal procession begin."

The crowd gasped when they saw the Emperor. Everyone had heard that only clever people could see his clothes.

"Aren't his clothes **splendid**?" they said.

"Let me see him!" called a small boy, who was stuck at the back of the crowd.

"Ooh!" said the boy. "The Emperor's got no clothes on!"

Faster than a spreading fire,
a whisper whizzed
through the crowd.

The Emperor's got no clothes on!

The Emperor's got no clothes on!

The Emperor heard their words. He looked down. "Oh no," he thought. "I'm naked!"

Then he blushed bright red.

"But I can't stop now. This is the royal procession and I am the Emperor." So he held his head high and walked on.

The crowd clapped and cheered. They thought it was the most splendid royal procession ever!

Meanwhile, Slimus and Slick were packing their bags full of money, getting ready to flee the palace forever.

A toast to invisible clothes!

"We tricked him!" they cried and cackled with glee.

Boris and the Emperor, of course,
weren't having such a good day.

But at least one thing turned out well for the Emperor.
People *did* talk about him for years to come...

The Snow Queen

Long, long ago,
and even further away,
lived two best friends, Gerda and Kay.

In all the world, no two friends were as close.

One crisp winter's day, Kay was crunching through the snow when he saw a twinkling snowflake.

It grew larger...

and larger...

until it turned into a woman, dressed in a sparkling white cloak.

The next second, she was gone.

But the following afternoon, while Kay was with Gerda... Ow! A speck of ice flew into his eye. From that moment, everything changed.

Kay began teasing Gerda and ripping up her precious roses. Then he made fun of people in the street.

As each day passed, he grew more and more horrible.

"Whatever's happened to Kay?" Gerda asked her grandmother.
Gerda's grandmother shook her head sadly and sighed.
"I think he's been enchanted by the Snow Queen."

163

After a while, Kay ignored Gerda altogether. He only wanted to play outside in the snow.

His cheeks glowed and his eyes shone.

He never seemed to notice the cold.

On the coldest day of the winter, the Snow Queen came for Kay.
In a daze, he caught hold of her sleigh.

She commanded her snow-white horse
in a voice spikier than icicles.

HOME!

And they flew from the market square, Kay clinging on behind.

The Snow Queen took Kay far,
far away, to her palace of ice in
the frozen north.

Kay grew colder, and colder, and colder...
so cold, he might have been carved from ice himself.

Week after week, he sat still as a snowman,
trapped in a room made from blocks of ice.

Soon, he completely forgot Gerda and everything in his old life.

But Gerda didn't forget Kay.

As the flowers started to bloom,
she set off to look for him.

First, she followed
the winding river.

When the river ran out, she left her boat and walked.
She walked for days and days...

...until, lost and alone in a forest, she finally stopped.

A glossy black crow hopped up to her. "Caaaaw," he croaked. "What's wrong?"

"I'm looking for my friend," she said. "The Snow Queen stole him."

"A queen?" croaked the crow. "Perhaps he's in the palace by the lake. Caaaaaaw. I'll show you."

He led Gerda through sleeping halls,
where royal dreams glided past.
"Try the robbers' castle," they
whispered. "Take the golden
coach outside."

171

The robbers' castle stood high on a hill,
stark against the sky.

Following a moonlit
path, the golden coach
rattled its way to
the top.

Inside the castle, Gerda told her story again.

"The Snow Queen lives in the frozen north,"
said a robber girl. "My reindeer can take you."

The robber girl watched them go, waving until Gerda and her reindeer were out of sight.

They had a long, hard journey ahead.

The air turned cold and stung Gerda's face like hail. Her face went numb but still they kept going.

At last, towering in the distance, she saw the Snow Queen's glittering palace.

In a whirl of snowflakes, the Queen's guards sprang at Gerda.

As Gerda cried out,
her breath formed
into misty angels.

Silently, they
swooped down and
attacked the palace guards.

Gerda ran into the palace calling for Kay.

She put her hand over his frozen
heart and it began to thaw.
A warm tear melted the speck of
ice in Kay's eye and trickled down
his cheek. "Gerda?" he whispered.

178

Kay jumped up, sending blocks of ice flying.
The Snow Queen could only watch in
icy fury, as Gerda and Kay fled,
leaving her chilly palace forever.

Back at home, Gerda's grandmother was overjoyed to see them. "I can't believe you escaped the Snow Queen!" she cried, over and over again.

And she hugged them both tightly, as if she'd never, ever let them go.

About the Authors

Aesop

Aesop might have been a wealthy man or a
slave – no one knows. All we do know is that some
of his stories, *Aesop's Fables*, were first told in ancient
Greece around 4,000 years ago. The stories are often
about animals and they always have a 'moral'
(a message or lesson) at the end.

Hans Christian Andersen

Hans Christian Andersen was born in Denmark,
in 1805, the son of a poor shoemaker. When
he grew up, he wrote hundreds of fairy tales
and became famous all over the world.

Lewis Carroll

Lewis Carroll was the made-up name of Charles Lutwidge Dodgson, who taught mathematics at Oxford University in England. He came up with the story of Alice during a boat trip, to amuse Alice Liddell, the daughter of a friend. It was published in 1865 as *Alice's Adventures in Wonderland*.

Carlo Collodi

Carlo Collodi was an Italian writer and schools' adviser, who lived over one hundred years ago. His real name was Carlo Lorenzini, but he used Collodi as his writing name, after the village of Collodi.

E. T. A. Hoffmann

Ernst Hoffmann was a writer and composer. He wrote *The Nutcracker and the Mouse King* in 1816. Nearly seventy years later, the composer Tchaikovsky used the story for his famous ballet *The Nutcracker*.

Cover and additional illustration by Simona Dimitri

Designed by Andrea Slane, Caroline Spatz,
Louise Flutter and Katarina Dragoslavic
Edited by Jenny Tyler

First published in 2010 by Usborne Publishing Ltd, 83-85 Saffron Hill, London EC1N 8RT, England. www.usborne.com Copyright © 2010 Usborne Publishing Ltd.
The name Usborne and the devices 🎈 🌐 are Trade Marks of Usborne Publishing Ltd.
First published in America in 2010. UE.